Weaving Imaginations

Flairs and Glairs

Publication House

"Weaving Imaginations"

ISBN No: " 978-93-90799-09-1"
1st Edition
Language – English and Hindi

Flairs and Glairs
Publication House
Regd. Under MSME Act.

Disclaimer

This is a work of fiction and solely represent the thoughts of the corresponding authors of the articles. Our editors have tried their best to edit the content of all the authors and check the plagiarism.

All the write-ups in this book are unique and are only published in this book.

In case any plagiarism or error is found, only the author is responsible alone, and not the publisher or the Compilers.

Cover Designing
Shubham Shah

Acknowledgement

First and foremost, we would like to thank the Almighty for the reason we are here today. We thank our Parents, Family, Friends and Every soul who helped us to make this book a successful one.

We thank Shubham Shah for giving us an opportunity and also for his constant support till the completion of the project. We thank Flairs and Glairs team for providing this wonderful platform for us and the budding writers.

We thank all the Co-Authors of this Anthology for being patient and keeping faith in us; co-operating, supporting and encouraging us in every step while making this Anthology. We would also like to give our thanks to the Designer, for coming up with such a wonderful cover page for this Anthology.

Preface

"Weaving Imaginations" is a book that deals with the different and unique imaginations one possesses, the creativity that grows within oneself, making them strive for better in life and make use of every opportunity they get effectively.

It also talks about the emotions rising from social issues or personal ones or even due to sudden incidents in life such happiness, fear, inspiration, or sadness caused by any tragic incident one faces in their lifespan.

The main aim of this anthology was to unite the young blood for a better change and unearth their creativity. It is an initiative to uplift the talents of such amazing individuals and provide a platform to showcase all the skills one can express through his/her words.

Flairs and Glairs Publication will always be grateful to its readers and above all the co-authors featured in the book. This anthology is a compilation of 42 writers across various states in India.

Co Authors

Shubham Shah (Founder Flairs and Glairs)
Ishani Agarwal (Co-Founder Flairs and Glairs)

1. Afrina Ahmed (Compiler)
2. Sahil Sk (Compiler)
3. Deepika Anchan
4. Devansh Singh
5. Aditi Tiwari
6. Anish Sardana
7. Sandeep Das S
8. Pritha Dey
9. Yashwanth Divi
10. Jharnashree Deka
11. Ujjwal Jha
12. Daka Tariang
13. Ruchi Nunia
14. Anoushka P S
15. Srijani Basu
16. Hiya Das
17. Priyanka Agarwal
18. Roshni Agrawal
19. Noor Ahmed Tamboli
20. Bhanuprakash Singh
21. Sneha Mukherjee
22. Diksha Reddy
23. Ashwini Venkatesh
24. Shrutika Patil
25. Athira Muraleedharan
26. Shaikh Abdul Wasee
27. Srotosini Acharyee
28. Divyataa Banerjee
29. Akrity Verma

30. Dr. Sakshi Pandey
31. Mr. Pradeep Kumar Pandey
32. Mrs. Sadhana Pandey
33. Sheikh Jamir Alam
34. Ankeeta Sahani
35. Samadrita Jana
36. Devashish Mandal
37. Radneswary Sooriyakumar Jegatheeswary
38. Sananda Bhattacharjee
39. Rashmi Maurya
40. Manisha Sharma
41. Ahana Debnath
42. Aashifa Rafiq
43. Swarnasankha Acharjee

Shubham Shah

(Founder- Flairs and Glairs)

Shubham Shah, an entrepreneur at "Flairs & Glairs" a brand with dynamics in events organizing and cultural educational pan INDIA, is a 26yrs old guy who recently has entered the digital platform of imprinting emotions. He has initiated with his own open mic platform to help budding poets and aspiring writers under his brand named as "Teekhe Zasbaaat"
He is a commerce graduate from the Bhagalpur City of Bihar.

He states Writing has impersonated him since childhood and he has now been writing for over a decade!

Cooking, on the other hand, is his passion! He also mentions, trying out new things just tickles him!

When asked sir, Why SPICY EMOTIONS?

He smiled and added, "agar jasbaat teekhe na ho toh wo jasbaat kahan" Spices are all that blends! So do his words!

As a chef, he presents to you his dish! Hot and freshly served! Taste it! Feel it! Enjoy it! You can also find his writing in the Book "Teekhe Zasbaaat" and 50+ Co-authored anthologies. With his passion to explore opportunities across Platforms, he is working with keen devotion and We wish him all the very best for his future ventures.

He is Featured in the **International Magazine De-Mode** for his upcoming solo novel.

He is **Approved by Ne8x for its Lit Fest,** and is a **Golden Star Awards 2020 Winner.**

He is an **India Book of Records Holder** for his Anthology **Satrang,** and has the **Grandmaster** title by **Asia Book of Records**, for the same.

He has also been featured in **Prabhat Khabar**, **Dainik Jagran** and other renowned Newspaper for his achievements. He has also been awarded with **India Star Republic Award 2021.**

He has been a proud co-author to

India Book of Records (Title- Black)

World Book of Records (Title -15 Wonders of Poetries)

India Book of Records (Title - Aaina)

Vajra World Records Holder (Title - Gustakhi Maaf Hai)

High Range of Records Holder (Title - Gustakhi Maaf Hai)

Share your reviews on his

Ishani Agarwal

(Co-Founder- Flairs and Glairs)

Ishani Agarwal hails from the City of Joy, Kolkata.
She is the co-founder of her Community "Teekhe Zasbaaat" and Flairs and Glairs Publication.
Been a Compiler for 45+ Anthologies, she is in the process for more. Co-authored in 150+ Anthologies. She is a India Book of Records Holder, a Vajra World Records Holder, a High Range of Records Holder and a Bravo Record holder.

Approved by Ne8x for its Lit Fest 2020, and Literary Icon 2020. Also a Golden Star Awards Winner 2020.

She has also been awarded with India Star Republic Award 2021.

She has been featured by the National Magazine "Taree Zameen Par" with the title 'unstoppable'.

Also featured in the International Magazine DeMode for her upcoming solo novel, she is proud to write on social issues, and is happy with the love she is receiving.

Connect with her on Instagram: @Ishani_agarwal_quotes / @compilations_so_far

Compilers Onboard

AFRINA AHMED

An ambitious girl with big dreams, the writer's name is Afrina aka Miss Affie♡. Hailing from Kolkata, her dream is to become a well-known Writer and Civil Servant.

"Men don't cry", they say, don't they have feelings too? Are they not humans, just like me and you? In "our society" boys have been taught not to cry, not to nag, not to be weak "like a girl". We question their masculinity every time they show their emotions. Is that right?I was going to the club that day with my best friend. Hardly had I known that my life would go crashing down that night. The club was crowded just like any other regular day. The dance floor was full of people. There was barely any space to even stand. My friend and I were drinking instead. I was thinking of my girlfriend, Niarina. Oh, how much I missed her! I've always been a loyal boyfriend. Yes, people did taunt me for being that way. I was asked time and again to hook up with random girls just to prove my 'manliness'. Never did I ever pay heed to that. I know I was attractive enough to be noticed at the first sight itself. I knew for a fact; I was getting a lot of attention from the females out there. My friend, Jake was already high. I knew I had to be under control just so I could take care of that mad ass! I made him sit on a couch. Exhausted, I sat next to him. I noticed a girl walking towards our direction."Hey hottie, want a drink?", She smirked.

"No thanks I'll suit myself", I retorted. Jake was way too high already. I helped him and took him to a room nearby. He kept blabbering and talking to himself.

"Dude shut up you're too drunk man", I yelled. I went out to get some fresh air. I took out my phone and was about to call up my girl. Suddenly, I felt someone tapping on my shoulder. It was that same girl!

"Heyyyy, wh- why are you ig- ignoring mmmmm me?", She said in a drunken state.

"Excuse me woman, you're not in your senses. Stop following me", I said. She took my hand and pulled me in her room. "What do you think you're doing?", I asked angrily.

"Shhh! You're going to love it boy", she said with a grin on her face. She forced herself on me. Ripping off my clothes she bit me here and there. She scratched me with her nails and thrusted her lips on mine. I, was in pain. I couldn't do anything to get out of the situation. I, felt helpless. She wouldn't let go of me unless she was done satisfying her lust. She was finally done and walked out. I, was left there with nothing to cover

my naked body. I was trembling in fear. Numb and quiet. I wanted to leave the place at once. I felt ashamed of myself for who I was. I knew no one would believe me. They would all question my "masculinity" if I told them what had happened with me. I had hallucinations after that day. I couldn't sleep nor could I eat. I was getting weak with every passing day. The guilt of not sharing what I had gone through, was killing me from inside. I didn't want to live anymore. I wanted to end things once and for all. My life, was a living Hell now. Would anyone even believe me if I told them I was raped? Would anyone stand by my side if I told them I'm a victim of rape too? That one night had changed my life, completely.

SAHIL SK

Hey there. Sahil this side! A guy head over heels in love with words. A writing enthusiast often preferring to write over emotions and abstracts than people. Coddiwompled my way over class 12 waiting for the results and currently hailing from Belur, West Bengal. Feel free to check my works and reach out at @a_moony_scriptwriter_ over Instagram!

Today I pen down melancholy for you.
When you read this work, I want you to feel subtle breathlessness, like a person in his chemo, dying everyday yet forced to stay.
I want you to lash out, break down, frantically look around for help and to your dismay find none like those in the
Russian Sleep Experiment and ultimately be something that your own reflection would dread.
Today I want you to suffocate but not die.
When you skim through these words, reminisce.
Reminisce all those moments when you didn't feel worthy and your death would have done a lot good.
Reminisce when everyone you knew looked away as you drowned with shrieks of deafening silence,
Reminisce all those days when you had everything and yet you let it all go because your conscience said, you had nothing,
Reminisce the truth in the statements when one said you, "Your existence does no one good."
Now as you feel disgusted, you skip words from my poetry, don't you?
I dare you not to leave.
I dare you to relive how sleepless nights were.
I dare you to caress your dead cold hands through the yellow stains your pillow cover harnesses, I dare you to switch your light lamp on and off,
On and off,
On and off, and wonder with closed eyes,
How days and nights are passing without your contributions, without your need in anyone's life, without you being you.
Are you weeping? I bet there's tears brimming if you read it thoroughly till now.
Are you? Then weep. Tear your eyes out.
Weep in lieu of the fact no one will shed tears when you pass away,

Weep like you did when your closest person tore your heart out and smirked at you. Weep like a tormented mother whose child succumbed at her very arms,
Weep like a person in OCD who wishes to rest yet is getting up for the 31st time to check the door lock,
Weep like people who lost their roof, like farmers who don't get food, like teenagers who let go their dreams.
Weep.
Now that I have broken you down.
We are on even terms. We are equal. We would be able to talk and not sympathize each other but empathize.
So, whoever's reading with utter difficulty for their tears veiling their vision,
I'm there too. We'll get through.

Co Authors Onboard

DEEPIKA ANCHAN

Software Engineer by profession and bibliophile by heart. She believes in perspectives and has a never give up attitude. "Spread love and not hate", "Live life Queen size" is her motto in life. Aspiring to be a writer of not so preferred genres soon!

Protectors of the realm,
Fighting day and night to safeguard their beloved.
Eliminating threats one after the other.
Easy as it seems, braving the nature's tantrums is
Nonetheless an ordeal.
There is nothing stopping them from bleeding their heart
out
In time of need.
Just like how a mother protects her offspring's,
They are the knight in shining armor for our nation.

DEVANSH SINGH

Raised in a Tier - 2 city in mainland Haryana, the dream of being a successful writer was always a little far-fetched and a big one. Now twenty years into existence, nine of which he has spent writing or trying to write poems, stories, prose, songs, the dream seems less far-fetched. He is learning as he writes, getting to know new things, trying to get better, much akin to humanity today. Hopefully you all will enjoy the process too.

Thundering cloud, deafening wind, a storm announced its arrival;
At the hospital a lady and her kid fought the battle of survival;
Hours went by, came the night sky, storm finally settled;
The battle was won with the setting sun, life had gambled;
There stood her dad who had never been so glad as he held his newly born daughter; "She'll have all I had with so much more to add!", now his eyes dropped water;
Time went by, that infant turned to a girl;
"She's so fierce!", "Have you seen her whirl?"
She had courage of her mother and was kind as her father;
Never used to shirk away, explored all that she could gather;
Judged, criticized, advised over and over;
"Behave like a girl!", "You can't be like this forever!";
But with her dad in her corner, mum being her supporter;
She broke the boundaries, her dreams and hard work hitting them like a mortar;
And away she flew into the mighty sky!
But sadly, that's where the vultures fly.

"They were worse than animals, do you know what did they do?";
I don't care! This is not a friggin' zoo!
And they weren't animals, they were humans who made their choice;
Who ravaged her, giving their inner Satan voice;
And no, animals were never this bad;
They dared called themselves "men", the living proof that God is dead.

"Rise and shine" is her motto "Organized with things and messy with thoughts"

He always keeps looking out of the window
I don't know why but I can foresee
Perhaps he likes the gusting winds which touch his face
When he slinks out of the window
Giving him a sensation of liberation to move
Hereabouts beyond like the winds, for they know no barriers,
He always keeps looking out of the window
As if he is doing all this for the end moment,
Trying to assimilate each and everything which foreruns him,
Because growth has its own constraints
He always keeps looking out of the window
As if he is going to heed the love of his life,
In the stranger's passer-by,
Who kens because as far as I assume?
We all rise as a stranger don't, we?
He always keeps looking out of the window
As if he knows how to fly the bogus mortal interaction
Because creation is the sole truth
He always keeps looking out of the window,
As if he knows that I am observing him
Because what he is looking is inside the window
And that's why he is candid to traverse
And as he continues to do this
I will keep on writing, "he always keeps looking out of the window"
For I embrace to presume …

ANISH SARDANA

A person who derives solace from writing. His aim is to connect with anyone who reads his poems, with only one message to give - Our differences are symmetrical. Instagram handle: symmetrical differences.

There are some pictures that we keep in our heart,
Some in front of us, some miles apart.
Unchanged for long, we keep them preserved,
Earning their true places which they deserved,
None at the top, none at the bottom,
Neither changing in summer nor forgotten in autumn.
Floating in our minds in the boundless ocean,
Each of them holds scores of emotions,
But how long does it take for a picture to change?
How long that the "friend" starts acting "strange"?
The picture is same but the person has changed,
In company of the "one" still feeling estranged,
Whom to complain about it, whom to blame?
We ourselves expect them to be the same.
Somehow the beauty of that moment alters,
The person in the picture somehow falters.
It is hard to accept these "unexpected" modifications,
But life does not run as per our specifications.
Old pictures may be replaced by the new,
But the ones unchanged
Still remain a few, still I keep some pictures in my heart,
Hoping to be in front of me, praying for miles apart.

SANDEEP DAS S

A graduate from apocalyptic era, who has too much time in his hand that weaves the magic of words to bring out the untold solitude we hide in our lives.
You can follow him on Instagram @das._.jr
Here is the link to his
bio

Are ghosts real? Or,
Is it just an illusion?
Is it because we dream? Or,
Is it because it exists?

We close our eyes, and
It feels like it is near us,
We try to touch it
But we forget its void.

We try to make effort.
Effort to find the ghost,
That we are dreaming of
In a hope that it is present.

We start dwelling on to it,
We start investing in it,
Just to reach the conclusion
That it is a dead end.

Is it memories of the person?
That we see closing our eyes.
Or, is it just another dream?
Which makes us think keen.

The human whom we used to see
Every day, every hour, every second
Is missing from puzzle of life.
Where did that person go?

Once in a while
It makes me think wild
If those humans existed in real
Or, is it just another unusual dream?

PRITHA DEY

She is a vibrant daydreamer, keeping her feet on the very reality. She is a believer. An art enthusiast, she loves enjoying the little moments with huge interpretations. She is simple and admires simplicity.

I love sour things
Sour food, sour love, but words!
As my fingers twitch to hold
the jar stuffed with tamarind pickles
My mother halts me and says,
'The scarlet gush from your golden pit
Shall rust the glass pot and break it into pieces.'
So, I touch it, but eat.

I turn the rose blemished pages of Veda
It says,
'Women took upon themselves
Indra's guilt of murdering a Brahmana
That befalls upon them every month
As impure crushed hibiscus wrath
And, thus blessed to bloom new seeds
A blessed curse, are we?

I love pious things
Pious food, pious love, but taunts!
As my fingers twitch to grab
the plate of sweets garnished as offering
My grandmother halts me and says,
'The cherry blossoms from down my tree
Shall pollute the metallic plate and break it into pieces.
So, I pollute it.

I ponder upon the legend of temple Kamakhya
It says,
'The sanctum sanctorum houses
The womb of Goddess Shakti and, bleeds
Of which the blood is cherished once a year
By people considering it pure.
No, I am not saying, I am your God
But I am mine.

And while I am penning this down
I bleed liquid vermilion in concurrence
Calling upon your God to banish me
As my God awaits along with me
Smoking a cigar amidst the red sea
You may call me an atheist.

YASWANTH DIVI

A vivid sage soul traveling to explore the unseen. Email id:

Why always did it start with friendship and ended with broken-hearted, red eyes and being strangers again? Yes, I love my best friend but what is my fault? It was always me who tried my level best to wipe out your tears and made you laugh when you were sad. Yes, I know I'm wrong, but what do you think, don't I stop me? Our love always caught me off guard. Do you know how my heart lurches with pain for you just to be with you? Do you ever try to understand my feelings? I always try to give you hints but I wonder do you ignore it or avoid it? I always hesitate to confess my love because I was too afraid to lose you. I'm shattered deep down but do you simply even care? I don't know how to erase you, how to delete your memories. I'm wounded, there are numerous scars you left behind. Each of them defines a story. Now we are strangers, but I still miss that favorite person of my life. Now my rainbow has become black. And the only thing left to ask is do you ever miss me? I miss you, my dear rainbow.

I don't know whether I matter in your life or not but I hope you remember me at least when you read this. I didn't know you; you didn't know me; we were completely strangers once but this universe conspired to made us meet. My smiles have been multiplying whenever I see you. Sometimes the most beautiful person is beautifully broken. Maybe we are not together now but whenever you feel sad, I'll be there for you to make you smile. I promise I'll never let you down. I am forever thankful that the universe conspired to make us meet. I Just caught myself smiling in every situation may be its because of you. Perhaps, we both have a lot of insecurities but they will never ruin our reliability. I am literally fond of you, your behavior your nature your personality and everything else that makes the imperfectly perfect you. You have changed my terrible life, by bringing in peaceful vibes. Believe me or not, but I could not find anyone better than you. I can't promise but I will always stay by your side, and hope you will too till the time

binds. More than anything you're my responsibility ♡. Your smile is permanent, I'll never get enough of it. From someone whom you met accidentally.

JHARNASHREE DEKA

Jharnashree Deka is a quarantine writer who developed her writing skills when she was free from her hectic daily scheduled life. Her credentials in writing poetry are based on the themes of love and life. Her educational background in literature has served as a base of her poems. One of her notable skills is that she could frame out phrases or quotes within a very short period of time regarding the reality of life. You can get her via Instagram: instagram.com/jharnadeka Email:

New classroom,
New beginning,
Also new flourishing bonds.
One took his seat,
Behind the other,
Just to take the introduction further.
Names got exchanged,
So as the phone numbers got too.
Virtual conversations kept on growing,
Concluding to meet in reality soon.
One fine day he decided to further the friendship,
Into the connection of love.
Thereupon the cafe across the street,
Turned out to be the destination,
To mark the dawn of a tender correlation,
Amidst two young hearts;
Where one confessed,
While the other accepted,
And bestowed the flower of love to bloom.

Life!
Real events along with real characters,
Where each and everyone plays their own roles,
In their respective factual events.
Where the themes might vary,
But struggles are the same.
Where the paths to attain the success,
Are imagined to be tranquil and trouble free;
But are much weirder,
Than portrayed in any piece of fiction.
Where every character is a protagonist,
Trying hard in their way,
To overcome the challenges,
And attain their peace of mind,
By achieving their desired aims.

UJJWAL JHA

Ujjwal Jha, a 20yr old Civil engineering student, is a resident of Jorhat, Assam. He started writing from the age of 10. He is a moody writer, he even likes painting, reading and learning technologies. He has also worked as co-author in some of the anthologies One can reach him at: ujjwaljha108@gmail.com IG Id.: ujjwal.dwg

It's been years now,
Time changed but my feelings
are still the same
Beards on my cheeks,
But you're not there to tease
Glasses on my eyes
But still can't find you,
Tears on my eyes
But they can't flow
You asked me to Smile
But you are not there to appreciate.
Now I've stopped promising,
Now no-one wishes me
Copperfield Morning.

अब दुनिया को खतम होते हुए देख रहा हूं
तुमसे दूर हो रहा हूं
सबसे दूर जा रहा हूं ,
मै नहीं मेरे देशवासी तड़प रहे है
पर में उनको तड़पता हुए देख रहा हूं,
शायद सही में अंत करीब हैं
वक़्त से परे हम सब हुए हैं डरे ,
सांस आती भी है तो डर कर ,
की कही जहर ना आ जाए,
सबसे दूरी बरत रहा हूं ,
ताकि वह हमारे करीब रहे,
सबको लगता हैं कि ईश्वर का कहर है
परन्तु यह हम मनुष्य द्वारा फैलाया जहर है।

She has a Master's degree in science and yet her achievement has always been her varied book collection.

I feel more at home in places far away from home.
I travel like I couldn't breathe, if I don't.
In the heart of this city with open doors,
My heart longed for yours.
I saw you standing adjacent to the front door of my hotel.
I usually choose hotels by the airport just to hear the sound of
airplanes fly by-
Just to quench my dear necessity to keep my feet and head up in
the sky.
You took my hand; we jumped into the cab.
We sat a few inches apart,
So couldn't hear the sound of my heart,
Beating so effortlessly just for you.
By the end of it all,
Your hands on my back,
I held your neck, in the back of the car,
Thrusting shadows and heavy scars;
I miss you
I miss the highway at midnight.
I miss the walks home.
I miss you tying my hair back.
I miss you looking at me.
I miss your hand under my sweatshirt.
I forget sometimes how easily you let me
Fall for you without you catching me.
I want to scratch your back out.
But you lost your way a while ago and I found my peace in your
distortion.

Five years later,
I still write paragraphs about you
And about how my home has always been,
With you.

RUCHI NUNIYA

Ruchi Nunia age 19 Comes from a small town 'Chirawa', Rajasthan. She is a college student, and also a sports person. She is a footballer and believes in hard work. Love to express her feelings by her creative poetry.

कुछ अधूरी सी है जो कहानी लिखी है ,
मैंने आज एक छोटी सी जुबानी लिखी है
करके इकट्ठी हमारी प्यारी सी यादें लिखी हैं ,
कुछ मीठी सी कुछ खट्टी सी बातें लिखी हैं
बारिश के बाद की रूहानी सी धूप लिखी है ,
खुशियों के सफ़र वाली कागज़ की कश्ती लिखी है
उन अंधियारों में खेली वो लुका छुप्पी लिखी है ,
एक था राजा एक थी रानी वाली सुहानी रात लिखी है
छोटी छोटी बात पर खाई माँ की हर डाँट लिखी है ,
पापा कब आएँगे ? इंतज़ार वाली शाम लिखी है
कुछ अधूरी सी है जो कहानी लिखी है ,
मैंने आज बचपन की जुबानी लिखी है

तेरे बारे में क्या लिखूँ, तूने तो ख़ुद मुझे लिखा है
तेरे आँचल को ओढ़ लू जो कभी , क्यूँ आता जन्नत का मज़ा है
तू करीब होती है तो सब सही होता है
तेरी गोद में सर रखकर हर गम दूर होता है
तेरा हाथों से सहलाना हर मर्ज़ की दवा बन जाता है
तू है तो ज़िन्दगी है , बिन तेरे जीना किसे आता है
रूठे जो कोई , झट से मना लेती हो
चोट लगे जो मुझे , क्यूँ अपना दर्द भुला देती हो कभी
कभी बड़ी चुप सी रहती हो
तकलीफ में हो पर पूछूँ तो सब ठीक है कहती हो
अंदर से टूटी हो पर बाहर से मुस्कुराती हो
मेरी गलतियों से नाराज़ हो , क्यूँ अपना गम छिपाती हो
गलतियों की सज़ा दो , क्यूँ सब सहती हो
अच्छा नहीं लगता ' माँ ' ज़ब तुम गुमसुम रहती हो

ANOUSHKA P S

Anoushka is a mental health advocate, aspiring writer, aspiring psychologist, social worker, content creator & multimedia blogger. She believes that to make a huge change in the world, you start by implementing small changes, one step at a time. She also believes that the qualities most looked up to in the world are empathy and kindness.

Some days I'm meaner than my demons. Simply because I am. I don't need to justify it. I carry both the pleasure of heaven & the pain of hell. I am what I am because of what's of my past. I chose not to accept the toxins of life. It was as if everything unpleasant in the world was a phone call, & I finally have the power to reject it. I take life as it comes, & enjoy the little things. I found that the best kind of happiness is the one I find in myself. My body knows me, she knows now that happiness comes not always easily. She knows you have to fight for what you love. She knows it's okay not be be okay. & some days when everything feels broken, she knows she's got to wake up & do what she loves even if in that moment she doesn't want to. She knows she's beautiful. She knows that curves come with edges, & edges can be beautiful too. She knows life is a ride, & it can get pretty messed up. But she also knows, that the mess can be beautiful if she wants it to be. She knows no emotion is permanent & no situation is either. She knows her want & her wills. Above all else, she knows she's all she's got.

That's what life is about after all. The endless possibilities of finding yourself. Not living the illusion that a bad situation gets better, but by making it better yourself. Not searching for love, but giving love to yourself. Because the only way to mend a broken heart, is to love it again. We all are just weary, pretty souls, in a single bonfire, the flame of some greater than others. That flame simply defined by passion. But sometimes all we need, is to just let it come as it does, & let things go as they do. To be so in love with YOURSELF, that it overcomes every possible hurdle. To love your scars & accept them too. More importantly, it's about knowing that every single soul, is trying to do the same.

SRIJANI BASU

Though engaged in a world of constants and variables, loves exploring the world full of pixie dusts and miracles.

Sometimes it scares me,
How much I wish to run away
From everything I have and everyone I know to somewhere;
Where I won't have to struggle to fit in,
Where I won't get tired of staring at the sky melting into the sea.

It scares me,
How much I want to find
Beauty and perfection in the imperfections of life, and
How much I want to dream
Of a love that stays.

It scares me, it scares me throughout
From being vulnerable to chasing dreams.
But,
In a world where we hope for a magic
That would bring our parallel universes closer to us, and
We would actually be in the places where we wanted to belong,
Then also,
Would we be all satisfied or
want more of everything?

I believe we would want more,
Because it's not always about what we have or what we want
Sometimes it's all about believing in things
That are out of our reach,
But having the comfort of knowing that it's there keeps us going.
"So, we'll just let things take their course, and never be sorry."-
F. Scott Fitzgerald.

HIYA DAS

15 years old, introvert. She loves poetry, and finds beauty in every form of art. Believes that we're born to break hearts.

They woke up to ashes and snow,
Looking for a way to escape.
They heard others roar
The same name again and again.

Wonder what was wrong with their heart
Buried their feelings in the dark
And yet, they feel so deeply
Hard to come out of the agony.

Ashamed of what they felt
Guilty for what they said
Tired of what they dealt
Wishing they were dead.

Listening to whispers only they could hear
Not knowing if it were even real.
Burnt down everything that were so dear.

Laid their heart on the blades
Knowing it would hurt
Knowing it would pain
Yet, they did so
Hoping to wake up to ashes and snow.

PRIYANKA AGARWAL

I m a teacher by profession. I have the passion for writing & sketching. Love to compose poems & quotes

ए मालिक मेरे प्रभु

क्या खूब दुनिया सजाई तूने

जिनको लाए हम इस दुनिया में

उन्होंने ही ना दी जगह किसी कोने में

खोई खोई सी जिंदगी में

कोई तो हमे धुंड ले

क्या कोई है ऐसा

जो हमारा हाथ थाम ले

उंगली पकड़कर चलना जिसे सिखाए हमने

नजाने वो आंखें कैसे तार रही हमें

इतना जोर कहां से आया उनमें

नजने वो आंखे कैसे ताड़ हमें

इतनी रोशनी कहां से आयी उनमें

कोई उन्हें बताए जरा

उन उंगलियों को रोकना भी हमें आता है

और वो आंखे जिनको हम सपने देखना सिखाए

उन आंखों को नीचा करना भी हमें आता है

क्यों ये युवा भूल गए

हम वही माता पिता है

जिन्होंने उन्हें तालीम दी

ये हमें ही तहजीब सीखा रहे हैं

और जिन्होंने छत के छाऊं दिए

ये उन्हें ही घर से निकाल रहे है

वृद्ध आश्रम भेजकर कहते है

यौर न्यू होम

शायद कहना चाहते हो

यौर लास्ट होम

बस प्रार्थना है यही

ए मालिक मेरे प्रभू

वो दुनिया भी खूब सजाने

जिनकी जिंदगी में नहीं

मां बाप का संग

ROSHNI AGRAWAL

She is Roshni Agrawal. She is from Delhi. Apart from writing she loves dancing and has deep interest in astrology too. Basically, she writes quotes, snippets and micro tales but she also loves to write poetry sometimes. She is a simple girl and a dreamer. She likes listening old songs. She lives with the philosophy of "live simple and keep your thoughts high". She had completed her graduation from Sophia College for Women from Mumbai. Being introvert, she thinks that writing is the best way to emote herself. You can find her on Instagram @just_being_spiritual.

Life is neither too short nor too long.
The moment in which we are living is life.
Every breath which we are taking is life.
Everyday which we are
Celebrating ourselves is life.
Our deeds and actions which we take is life.
Doing those things which
Makes us happy is life.
Life is described by the way of your living.

Tips to raise your vibrations: -
1) I am healing.
2) I have come a long way.
3) I am doing pretty well at my pace according to my capabilities.
4) Before going to bed pray to god and thank him for everything. Instead praying to remove your sorrows, pray him to give you strengths to overcome and heal from it.
5) Stop complaining and criticizing instead start appreciating little things in your life.
6) Think life is not hard and difficult as it seems to be.
7) I am learning.
8) I can do it.
9) Carry love in your heart and be generous in your givings.
10) Set a positive intention before going to bed.
11) Write down those things which you are grateful for.
12) I am working on myself.
13) Positive self-talk. Self-talk because you are not just talking to yourself but also you are talking to your inner-self and soul. Your soul is linked to god.

Practice these affirmations for self-love and let your vibrations speaks louder than your words.

NOORAHMED TAMBOLI

"From a city called Bijapur often cited as the hottest city in Karnataka, he loves catastrophe, kind of a loner and adores his own company, a self-proclaimed pessimistic but doesn't quit wishing or dreaming, frequently caught in the middle of the diplomacy - cherishes honest direction, He is a movie maniac and hardcore tv-series binge-watcher, loves reading tragedy, thriller, and a fictional genre novels, his all-time favorite writers are JK Rowling, Mitch album, and John Green".

Slumbering on the floor
Dreading about life before,
I remain awake most of the nights,
like that feeling of a vacant spirit,
Yeah, I breathe a little different,
stroll around pretending that everything is perfect,
when I skate through the streets,
the empty stalls and stores,
Visualizing the flowers on my grave,
The memoranda from the people who executed me with their
sharp tongue,
I drink a lot of liquor,
take pills to fight the terror,
carving and cutting has become my pleasure,
peek at the paintings in my home,
They howl the suffering due to colors itched on them,
I loathe the normal,
The trauma that has caused,
doesn't let me be Nobel,
Often find solace in selling body,
Oh no that's not a girl trend,
We are sexist in some kind,
Wander through the guilt,
Few bucks that were paid,
Often rehab is the territory I end,
I like the green grass,
Polished within not meant to eat,
When headlights hit your sight,
the roads don't seem honest,
Parading on the highway is exhausting,
throwing up your guts out isn't so soothing,
When you fade due to curses,
It's dangerous to survive,
Living on the supply that meant to destroy,
You skip the things that brought you pain,

Adore the blood that cuts through wings,
decided to fly in sufferings,
Without realizing that your drowning.

BHANUPRAKASH SINGH

Bhanuprakash Singh is an engineer by profession, and a writer by passion. A deep interest in philosophy and nature keep him engaged. Discovering himself through his writings, strumming his guitar, and filling a blank canvas with colours is what he loves. He wishes that his thoughts, through his writings, help his readers discover their inner selves too!!

We are not above anyone,
and neither is anyone alone.
When we see each one prone,
to what they are destined to own,
we know that this is to hone,
every life to that purpose alone,
to which one here is born!

This universe has a way long,
to shape the thoughts strong,
and to mould the days along,
in a way that never goes wrong.
And to that secret we belong,
which makes us one day strong,
to which one here is born!

We come, we go, but this lawn,
is here to house us all among,
and has all care to us drawn,
while we hand in hand bring on,
happiness around every dawn,
spreading each smile among,
to which one here can be born

When I began my day today,
I had a hope urging to say,
that I can make it unlike yesterday,
and can race ahead come what may.
That the best is now, along the way,
and no one's taking that away!!
When I worked long like every day,
I had a desire urging to pray,
this time, I deserve, above they,
and my effort's going the right way.
That I will be known, the best one day,
and alike past, let see no betray!!

When I lay back at the end of the day,
I had a wish urging to stay
close to what is peace, my soul say,
and to that my heart longs, every day,
far from that, which keeps happiness away,
and in the small smiles, unknown that sway!!

SNEHA MUKHERJEE

58

Sneha Mukherjee is a senior school student with a great passion of writing. She is a well-rounded individual who lives with passion, dedication and grace.

We're lost souls
Searching for love
Wandering in the streets we have never been to
Searching for the people we've never seen
Hoping for the dreams that won't come true

Every time the clever mind gives us a jerk
To tell us that it won't be true
Those dreams won't take place
The love of your life will not even look at you
Every time it tries to warn you
Not to repeat the same mistake again

The broken yet stubborn heart
Shouts louder than the mind
Gives you pain though some relief from the anxiety
outside
And tells you that
Yes, it can be true
Yes, you can get the person you love
Yes, your dreams can be achieved
And you believe it again
And you fall
You fall and there's no one to hold you up
There's no one to take you back home
You get trapped in your own abyss
You get trapped in the street lights
And the crowd

You forget the songs you heard
You forget to smile
Because you are more familiar to grief now

You forget to make your present beautiful
Because you're still not able to overcome your past
And that is when you think about your mind
You think about the things it said
You think about the warnings it gave you
And you slowly you start following it
Gradual but fruitful
You don't look back at your heart because you know you
it might break you again
You are strong now,
Stronger than yesterday
And every single day you felt yourself to be weak.

DIKSHA REDDY

Hey fellas, this is Diksha Reddy, a typical South Indian 'not so teenager' born in a traditional family. She is currently pursuing her degree in Bengaluru- The Silicon Valley. She loves her audience and will definitely appreciate your views, either positive or negative, which you could leave her at

The sky and earth showed what they were like:
The Earth craving furiously with a strong strike
The Sun hampered, devastated and turning hoist
Growing wide and wild in the silent noise

A house appeared in the blink of an eye
I understood that the end was nearby
With the eyeballs enlarged and horrified
I was trying to focus on the other side

But as I sleep there quietly and gaze
There I could see an endless space
Still beyond, there was more than earthly life
And this phase is definitely an expected rife

Suddenly my vision went off the sight
Everything seemed like a pitch-black night
I was struggling there sleeping on the couch
And I refused going until someone vouch

Meanwhile I saw an angel in the sky
With the open wings she started to fly
Slowly turning around, she looked at me
With a little smile she said, "It's time to flee."

ASHWINI VENKATESH

Hello!!!! This is Ashwini Venkatesh, she belongs to a traditional south Indian family. She is a co-author of this book and she is pursuing her degree yet in Bengaluru. Her hobbies are writing, listening songs. She started writing to express her thoughts and share it with others. She would appreciate the reviews and the reviews can be left at her email .

Dear soul I know how hard it is
To just stand still like a mannequin
After all the hurdles you had to face within
But this is the battle we have to fight and win

Traction won't help us for sure
But my kin tranquil is the solution to cure
Just know the deflation is not endure
As the skirmish have to be won by wisdom of yours

Buck yourself up for more
Hakuna Matata, as you are rigid from the core
We will surely reach the final shore
As this is the battle that have to be fought for reasons more

For you are stronger than the throb
Smirk is the best way to fight for sure
As hope is what I feel is the best cure
And this is the letter that I had to give to my soul.

Oh, there I stand so alone
Just quiet and blown
In the world filled with faces unknown
Calming myself by saying everything's for a boon

I swoon is this world for real
I see only masks and that isn't a big deal
Keeping mum isn't a proper heal
For I think to fill the void shrewd is the correct seal

I suppose weak is staying lone
But no! fake camaraderie however gets flown
Dopamine is released as I bloom
Adrenaline rushes as the truth is known
Oh, it's better to stay away from the unknown
And that's why I stand there safe and alone....

SHRUTIKA PATIL

Blooming writer searching for the ounce of dynamism!

It's been a while since I have written about anything. But today is different, I am having an unstoppable urge to pour that viscous fluid filled in my brain onto the paper. And the funniest part is even I don't know what it is about. Is it going to be just another illusion my mind is playing with me? Or is it going to be an outburst of what is kept inside for so long? Or is it going to be really meaningful which can change my perspective about things? I don't know.

When they talk about love they say that it's something which is irreplaceable, unconditional and selfless. But the truth is, it has the conditions, always. Over time you will realize that what you were looking for is just a mere and you will start accepting the modified definition of love created by this modern world. And acceptance is never an easy deal, especially when it comes to something which you have always believed. You will settle for less; you will start to think that this is what you deserve. But what you will never realize is that you can't go along with your beliefs altered. It's going to leave a void inside you and you will be tired trying to fill that void.

But the worst part is when you stop believing in yourself. When you start thinking that you are just too much for everyone. When you are already in a storm, damp, and freezes you can't expect someone to dance with you in your storm. Nobody wants to let your hurricane into their hearts. People need a breeze to comfort their tormented souls, and definitely not the hurricane which can destroy them. When you open your true feelings to someone, in the hope that they will have the courage to fight with you, but rather they get scared and choose to leave the war.

You can't rely on someone to wipe away your dried tears. This world doesn't need to see your cries which nobody ever heard. After all who is going to take efforts to see through that darkness? There is no guardian angel and nothing like the knight in the shining armour. It's your war and you have to keep fighting.

But does this have to end? Yes of course. Every war has an end no matter if you are the only one fighting. and the end is when you will accept that you are incapable of loving. It's harsh but it's the fact. And someday you will accept it with no regrets. You will find yourself in a position where the only thing left will be you, blaming yourself for what you made yourself do. You will have immense love to give but you won't be able to give any. You will crave for someone so badly, there will be no signs of them returning.

I wish if this war goes on for a life and never ends. Not everything ends in a pleasant way. I wish that whoever is fighting this war will wake up one day feeling empowered by the parts of themselves that at one time they had labelled as flawed. I hope that they will keep loving the stars till one of them decides to fall for them!

ATHIRA MURALEEDHARAN

Athira, an artist who accidentally became a writer. Started writing about her every day crushes, she fell in love with! From then she had an exciting journey writing more about romance and lust. The story here is very close to her heart. Writing has helped her gain very personal access to the outside world. Inspecting people from different angles and making tales of her own about love in a world full of love!

My semester was about to end.

It was finally time for a summer internship.

I was pursuing a Masters in Mass Communication and Journalism down south.

I was excited to travel back home for summer vacation. I had my reason to be happy. Finally, I reached home and shouted with glee, "Maa...... I got an internship offer from a media house. I will soon be traveling to Mumbai!!!"

My parents looked worried and tense but faked a smile.

I understood their concern but didn't want to miss the opportunity.

One week past, it was time to leave for the city of dreams as Mumbai is certified.

My dad accompanied me to Mumbai, got me a safe place to stay, and left.

As I updated the event on Facebook a messaged popped. It was my best friend Archana.

We were put up in the same grad school. After graduation, we never really met. The last time I had a chat with her she was working in Delhi as a Software engineer.

The message read "Hey, how come you landed in Mumbai!!"

I went on and explained the whole story of the internship and how excited I'm to work in the media firm.

And my happiness doubled when Archana told me that she will be flying down to Mumbai to attend a meeting and will be here for a week.

My happiness knew no bounds. After all we were meeting after 1.5 years.

Days passed and my internship was shaping up well. Good team, good people, and a lot of stuff to learn. I was thoroughly enjoying my part there.

Finally, the most awaited part came. The arrival of Archana.

I was excited to see her after so long.

As planned, I left early from the office. Boarded a local train and headed towards Bandra.

I searched for a good coffee shop and found one.

It was a classy cafe with all the dim lights and fancy tables.

I checked in and texted Archana the location.

While I scrolled through my Instagram, I felt like someone is looking at me.

I glanced through the room and saw a guy in the corner.

I wasn't prepared for something unexpected to happen.

The guy didn't look creepy so I remained unbothered.

I was back in scrolling the Instagram again and suddenly this guy walks to me.

I got a bit nervous, but what he whispered I will never forget.

He simply stood by me and whispered, "You are irresistible like dark chocolate"

He looked into my eyes, smiled, and walked away.

He left me blushing.

Then, Archana came and gave a tight hug. I was happy to see her but this man kept hovering my mind for good.

That unknown man in a new city gave another reason to love me for who I am. For a dark girl like me, getting a compliment with no ifs and buts felt so authentic that it touched my soul.

This remains the most cherished moment till date!

Writer by circumstances, not by choice.

As the title of this book suggest which is weaving imaginations. Imagination is slightly similar to that. Because our imagination has no limit whereas threads have. Our imagination can be an endless loop or a never-ending tunnel. It all depends on our perspective. When your mind creates a world of its own, that world is build on the fragments you capture in reality which lead to difference of the factors that affect your imagination. A person who has always been working imagines or desires a vision in his mind of a world without so much hustle and more rest and peace. If a person who has been in four walls all the time, creates how the world would be on the other side of the wall. The world outside those four walls can be dark and scary, and if the person imagines and perceives that part, eventually he or she ends up being scared of it and makes it his or her choice to be confined to those walls for perpetuity but if he creates or believes in his imagination of the wad which is basically good and based on humanitarian grounds ends up believing in good and even behind those four walls, that person doesn't lose hope to see that world one day. So that's what imagination does to our mind and eventually body, if you don't imagine about a good physique or desire a good lifestyle then you might not work for it and that push to do the work is caused by imagination. You might cook some recipe even when you are amateur at cooking just because you imagine yourself eating that particular dish and feel the need to try or find it tasty in your imagination. So, imagination does make you do things. Imagination does create difference by not even participating in the actual reality we live in by making us see ourselves see the consequence of our actions in the fabricated reality we create on our own. So maybe it's true that what we imagine, we become.

SROTOSINI ACHARYEE

A UPSC aspirant that she is with keen interest in politics and sports alike, Srotosini also has a flair for writing. A Potterhead and a Holmes fan, she gets hooked into fiction like a regular latte. She is currently in 11th standard, excelling and flourishing her abilities in Humanities. She loves dogs more than humans but, socialization is what she demands in a full-fledged party.

I don't know, what makes me so worried,
Is it the pain of losing you?
Or is it the memories that do not want to fade?
I don't know, what makes me so ecstatic,
Is it that you still remember me?
Or is it that you would eventually come back for me?
I don't know, what makes me so heartbroken,
Is it that I will never see you again?
Or is it that you may be happy in someone else's arms?
I don't know, what makes me so alone,
Is it the loneliness that you left me with?
Or is it just the vacancy of my room?
I don't know what makes me so angry,
Is it that I could never love you enough?
Or is it that I was too much obsessed about you?
I don't know why you left me,
Why you inflicted such pain,
Because no matter how much I loved you
Unaccounted for, it was all in vain.
I tried to understand you, wanted to give you my world,
But you never let me understand,
It was difficult to love a wounded heart.
Yet, I love you,
I love you with all my heart,
No matter how much it pains
I will always do!
Because you are the one who made me understand,
Love wins when only your ego fails.

DIVYATAA BANERJEE

Bubblish. Ambivert. Head full of dreams. Self-taught chef and video editor. A National Level Story Teller. See's the world through rose coloured glasses.

एक बच्चा क्यूँ रोता है?
शायद माँ ने फिर से आज उसे डाँटा है।
शायद रात के अंधेरे में वो डर सा जाता है।
शायद उसको समय पर खाना नहीं मिल रहा है, या शायद वो कच्ची
नींद से उठ गया है।
माँ को भी कुछ समझ नहीं आ रहा है, कि बच्चा क्यों रो रहा है।
शायद बहुत सी वज़ह हैं।
पर शायद वो "अंकल" आज फिर आए थे।
एक बच्चा शायद इसीलिए रोता है।

The day was beautiful,
And she died.
Under the sky,
On the green sheet.
She lay.
Everybody asked,
Bow did she die?
A normal cold and cough,
Maybe pneumonia, I lied.
She had visited the mirror that day,
And all her insecurities came her way.
Not just a little chubby,
And those freckles as well,
Rather shy...
Quite ordinary in a way.
Maybe she should have known,
She didn't have to fit in the
Predetermined mould...
Maybe she'll find peace up there,
Where no one will judge her once again.
The day was beautiful,
And she died.

AKRITY VERMA

Hello everyone, I am Akrity From Ranchi, and I have completed my graduation in 2018, I love to write Poem and Short stories, basically I am writing on the topics of Love Romance and sometime social issues, I also like singing, dancing, sketching, cooking and gardening. I love to read novels and listen Podcasts of stories.

पत्तों की झड़झड़ाहट में उस रोज एक अलग ही साज़ था....
छतों से टपकते हुए बूंदों का भी अपना एक अलग ही राग था....

याद है उस रोज के अफसाने.....
कैसे पिघल रहे थे हम दोनो परवाने....

हर तरफ संगीत ही संगीत था....
मेरे होंठों पे केवल तेरा ही गीत था....

हवाएं भी अपनी अलग ही कहानी कह रहे थे....
हरे हरे नजारे भी कुछ अलग इशारे कर रहे थे....

सावन भी आज अपनी मोतियाँ लूटा रहा था....
फूल बेलियों के महीनो के प्यास मिटा रहा था....

लाल गुलाबी अनेको रंग बिखेरे जा रहे थे.....
मानो हम दोनो को ही मिलाने के लिए साजिश रचे जा रहे थे.....

चिड़ियाँ पेड़ो पे बैठे गीत गुनगुना रही थी....
चमकती बिजली भी हमें डराकर पास ला रही थी.....

न जाने उस रोज मौसम को क्या आस थी....
मैं सोचकर इतरा रही थी कि मैं तेरे पास थी....

मौसम के जादू में मैं इतनी घुल रही थी....
मुझको भनक भी न लगी सांझ ढल रही थी....

पास रह जाऊँ हरदम के लिए माँग रही खुदा से यही मन्नत थी....
तेरे बांहों में मुझे मिली जन्नत थी.....

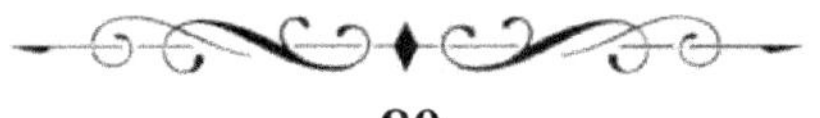

DR. SAKSHI PANDEY

Dr. Sakshi Pandey, a girl of jovial personality is a Dental Surgeon and a Clinical Cosmetologist by profession and a Writer by passion. She got inspired by her parent's written poems and developed love for writing during early childhood. She has performed at various popular events and considers Mic as her permanent bae. Using 'Pravarshi' as her pen name, she believes in pouring raw emotions in her pieces as her motive is to help people by touching their heart through her writings. Humanity attracts her the most. Apart from this, she enjoys traveling, exploring and loves animals.

Those who possess the true starvation,
Have the zeal to achieve their destination,

To live their dream, their soul strives,
And for them, the wheel of fortune smiles.

Those who care with innocent childlike heart,
Those who accept failure, only to give a fresh restart,

They search for truth, even in this world full of lies,
And for them, the wheel of fortune smiles.

Those who spend time in appreciating nature's beauty,
Selflessly they keep performing the divine duty,

Omens help them to cover the satisfactory miles,
And for them, the wheel of fortune smiles.

Those who believe in helping the sufferers,
Those who always remain queer travelers,

Happiness is what their life implies,
And for them, the wheel of fortune smiles.

Those who enjoy simple things without complication,
Ocean's depth, fragrance of blossoms, laughter of children,

Their jolly life brightens like star filled skies,
And for them, the wheel of fortune smiles...

Make sure your wheel of fortune is also smiling.

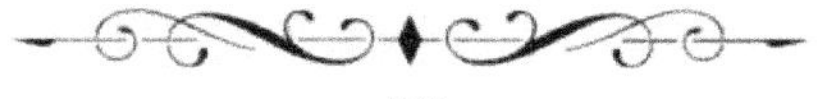

MR. PRADEEP KUMAR PANDEY

श्री प्रदीप कुमार पाण्डेय जी वर्तमान में एक प्रतिष्ठित ऑटोमोबाइल कंपनी में सीईओ पद पर कार्यरत हैं। इन्होंने इंजीनियरिंग एवं मैनेजमेंट में डिग्री हासिल की है। वे काव्य एवं गद्य दोनों ही विधाओं में समान रूप से लेखन कार्य करते रहते हैं। धर्म विज्ञान समाज तथा अध्यात्म सभी विषयों का विवेचन तथा अपने जीवन की अनुभूतियों का चित्रण उनकी लेखनी में सहज रूप में दृष्टिगोचर होता है। छात्र जीवन से ही इन्होंने वाद-विवाद प्रतियोगिताओं और अनेक सांस्कृतिक कार्यक्रमों में प्रथम स्थान अर्जित किया है ये बहुमुखी प्रतिभा के धनी विनम्र और उच्च व्यक्तित्व के विचारों वाले कवि हैं। पवन उपनाम से लेखन कार्य करने वाले प्रदीप जी ईश्वर के अनन्य भक्त हैं जिन्हें अनेको लोग अपना आदर्श मानते हैं।

उलझन, बेचैनी, नीरसता, अवसाद घनेरे घिरे हुए।
हैं देते आमंत्रण प्रतिपल तड़पन से भरे जीवन के लिए।।

यह तड़प विवशता से पूरित लाचार बना कर रखती है।
क्यों विशद वेदना पैदा कर यह शांत नहीं रह सकती है।।

जो तड़प रहा उससे पूछो वह घोर कष्ट में जीता है।
वह जीते जी ही मरा हुआ अपने को अनुभव करता है।।

वह श्रेष्ठ मृत्यु को पाता है अविरल विराम चाहता है।
वह चिर निद्रा व महाप्रयाण को सदा सुखद ही पाता है।।

स्पंदित गति से दूर विरामित शांत प्रदेश का जीवन।
बरबस उसे लुभाता मचलाता इठलाता और कहलाता।।

है यही सत्य और महा सत्य जिसमें न तड़पना होगा।
जीवन में उल्लास हर्ष उत्साह प्रेम रस होगा।।

शाम का वक्त था अंधेरे का धुंधलका छाता जा रहा था वातावरण में,
रेल गाड़ी चली जा रही थी
अपनी रफ्तार से ग्रामीण अंचल से शहरी गंतव्य की ओर।
तथाकथित विकास मार्ग पर सहसा
एक अत्यंत भोली भाली सरल तरुणी ने
आकृष्ट कराया मन को खिड़की के बाहर के दृश्य की ओर,
जहां उठ रही थी लपटें आग की खेतों एवं खलिहानों में
नवयौवना बाला ने मुझसे पूछा यह आग क्यों लगाई गई है
मैंने उत्तर दिया-
सफाई की जा रही है खेतों की जलाए जा रहे हैं खरपतवार।
शांत सरल किंतु बुद्धिमता पूर्ण ढंग से बताया उस युवती ने आग लगने
का कारण
वह बोली यहां पर प्लॉटिंग की जानी है इसलिए लगाई जा रही है एक
भयंकर आग प्राकृतिक वनस्पतियों में
गांव से शहर एवं असभ्य से सभ्य बनने के नाम पर।
।

MRS. SADHANA PANDEY

श्रीमती साधना पाण्डेय प्रयागराज विश्वविद्यालय से दर्शनशास्त्र एवं हिंदी विषयों में स्नातकोत्तर हैं। वह एक ग्रहणी और समाज सेविका हैं। वह धार्मिक विचारधारा से ओतप्रोत आधुनिक वातावरण को सहज रूप में आत्मसात करने वाली तथा जीवन को साधारण रहते हुए भी आनंद और उल्लास पूर्ण रूप में जीने की चाह रखने वाली महिला हैं। उनकी लेखनी में त्वरित भावों एवं विचारों को समाहित करके प्रस्तुत करने की क्षमता दिखती है।

रवि शशि नयन तेज में भासित,
वृक्ष रूप में स्वयं विराजित।
पक्षी गगन पुंज आह्लादित,
बागों में भंवरे गुंजारित।

सर में लाल कमल दल शोभित,
सावन में हरियाली मोहित।
सुर लय ताल सकल में सुरभित,
सहज सरल पावन में विकसित।

पुष्प बहार स्वयं में प्रमुदित,
शिशु की किलकारी में पुलकित।
वन उपवन वाटिका प्रफुल्लित,
ग्रीष्म उमस में शिशिर प्रवाहित।

जलधि उच्च लहरों में गर्वित,
गिरि शिखरों में हिम आच्छादित।
तन समीर जीवन संचारित,
वातावरण फुहार सुगंधित।

वाणी में अमृत वचनामृत,
जल में मृदु शीतलता स्वादित।
धरा समस्त जगत को धरणित,
वेद पुराणों में शुभ वर्णित।

गहन तमस में भी उज्ज्वालित,
अग्नि प्रचंड हवन प्रज्वालित।
जीव जीव में सकल समाहित,
कण-कण में प्रभु तुम प्रतिपादित।

वीणा के तारों में झंकृत,
ॐ स्वस्ति श्री रूप अलंकृत।
भक्ति भाव आनंद स्पंदित,
सर्वव्याप्त हरि तव उर वंदित।

SHEIKH JAMIR ALAM

Sheikh Jamir Alam is a Senior school student who takes up 3d art as a hobby. He believes that art can bring people together and help them grow. He wishes to be able to share his stories and imaginations in the form of his art.

Is it necessary to act like other couples?
Is it necessary to go to different places?
Is it necessary to act all lovey-dovey?
Can't we sit at home and talk?
If you love me, then anything we do together is fun right?
I love you; I don't love to act.
So, if you love me, you don't have to pretend.
I wonder, what will lead me to happiness;
Doing what is right,
Or, doing what I want.

ANKEETA SAHANI

Ankeeta Sahani is a Creative Artist & a Community Radio Jockey from Odisha. She loves to convert the real-life stories into beautiful tales. Her own written Poems & short stories are the reflection of another side of the same coin. She is born on 09.09.2001 & brought-up in the city of Culture "Sambalpur". Insta/fb: @ankeetaas Mail Id:

आंखे थकने लगी हैं मेरी
मैं अब भी जाग रही हूं
पलके झुकने लगी हैं मेरी
मैं अब भी ताक रही हूं

मैं जरा सी रोशनी की चाह में
नज़रे गड़ाए बैठी हूं,
गुजर जाएंगी ये आज की मुश्किलें
मैं आश लगाए बैठी हूं

इंसाफ होगा मेरे जज़्बातों के साथ
भरोसा है मुझे उन खयालों पर
भरोसा है मुझे अपने इरादों पर

कुछ इन्हीं उम्मीद के साथ
मैं अपनी बाहें फैलाए बैठी हूं
मैं नए कल के इंतजार में
अपनी सांसे सजाए बैठी हूं

कब से हार कर खुद से
में इन राहों को देख रही हूं
आंखे थकने लगी हैं मेरी
मैं अब भी जाग रही हूं
पलके झुकने लगी हैं मेरी
मैं अब भी ताक रही हूं

SAMADRITA JANA

Samadrita Jana, hailing from Kolkata, India, is currently pursuing medical studies in the Philippines. When she isn't trying to remember scientific names and a thousand reactions in vain, she loves to read and write. Dancing and creating art have been her passions from ever since she can remember. She prefers food, flowers and animals over people any day, and honestly longs to see a world filled with love and kindness.

She stumbled upon the word just like she stumbled upon so many precious things in her life, hidden away in ruffles of the pages of a book she had just picked up, from the dark corner of the library where nobody ever went and even the librarian shot her furtive glances, trying hard every day to veer her towards the bestselling section or even the young adult section once in a while.

But she never thought of herself as belonging there, she never did; in reality, she knew she would always find her way back to the stories that sat upon the shelves in darkness, gathering dust, unread by all, for she was home there, sometimes she wondered if someone was always watching her, from the shadows, lurking behind as she took every step in her life and then creating something so beautiful and magical; stringing all the words between the covers, pages after pages, making her excuse for a life seem like the most powerful existence in the world. She wished more people would read those words and feel their beauty, but then again, she revelled herself in owning those words, almost didn't want them to see the light; for she found comfort in them, in the darkness of the corners, in being in a world where nobody ever entered, where everyone was scared they would encounter their deepest darkest fears, where the world stopped being black and white and started being gray.
She looked up the word, and she felt like it was hers. All the books and the websites labelled it as a condition, for her, it was just a way of life. It was the first time she felt like she wasn't alone, the alone that she felt every time she told her best friend that she wished she could just slip into darkness without anyone knowing, and her best friend would freak out thinking she was having suicidal thoughts. She wasn't, mind you, she wanted to live every single second of what the world had to offer to her, but she wanted all of those seconds in her own way. Or the alone she felt every time she asked her brother

why he was so cheerful when he witnessed the sunrise when nothing could be as beautiful as the night, with its darkness, engulfed in silence, when she could feel every moment of it coursing through her veins, her heart beating fast, when it was the only time she ever felt alive, only for the night to be over too soon; did nobody else ever notice how it just passes away in the blink of an eye?

But ever since she came across the word, she couldn't have been happier; there was nothing that could make her feel alone, ever again. It was her word, almost as if a sculptor had looked at her and saw the magic that she so desperately wanted to see in herself, wanted to believe that she had inside her; and wanted to keep her forever, in a string of letters that she hoped, one day, would show its magic to the world, just like it did to her. She hoped that, one day, like her, her brother would see that the night, with its darkness and its silence, made every sunrise more beautiful than ever, you just had to embrace the night as your own to feel its beauty. She hoped that her best friend would, one day, be brave enough to face her fears and scars, and finally see how slipping into the darkness would make her see her own beauty more than ever. She knew, that all the world was just waiting for the right time to slowly fall into the abyss, the great dark nothingness that had been beckoning us since forever, to slowly slip into the darkness that was her home, to stop being black and white and start being gray; for she knew, that even though everyone wasn't brave enough to embrace it and believe in it, all of them saw their true selves at night, they found their comfort in the darkness, it made them feel alive, more than they ever felt, and she knew that like a drug, its magic would slowly seep into every person's veins, and make them see beauty in their own little ways.

For ever since she found the word, she has never felt alone, because; she felt the whole world slipping into and finding happiness in the darkness, into her home, and if that was true

and the whole world was her home, then wasn't the whole world a nyctophile, just like her? And in that moment, she felt infinite, and at one with all the darkness around her, for, finally, she was home.

DEVASHISH MANDAL

Pen name- Itchy mind. He is a critical reader. Dedicated and supporter to cause. He believes in appropriate response than spontaneous reaction.

I remember some I was a toddler, was a war hero stepping out of cradle.

All that is fine arrangement of spectaculars. I was the crown stone of whole carnival. Some played games, played and became game.

Years passed and so did the time.

There wasn't time to play but surrounded by players in disguise and life competence to unfold the winner.

I chose to be loyal and ethical in all my whereabouts. But there were half-breeds, grim, loss and distress is all they feed around.

I screamed in fright, If I wasn't rival than why should I defend a fight.

They came and stripped off my virtue

And disgust mutilated my dignity.

I begged my breath.

But they pour the poison of threat.

All ridiculed of my bare tender self.

I was captivated among wolves and hyenas waiting for their slice.

In the end I could feel my soul dying and i closed my eyes.

Then as I recommence my vision, I couldn't recognize myself.

As if identity kept in records of shelf.

What pained couldn't destroy me.

What retained couldn't represent me.

What I went through anymore couldn't torment me.

There was no honour in vengeance.

There was no hope to rebel.

There was no sense in calling of guidance.

There was no resentment in this shell to reside.

But once a player still remains a player.

Put a mask and cape just a bit like layer.

Now beware of me and get off my way.

I am not hurt to hurt anyone who frays.
Now perhaps my words taste salty.
Trust me it's just part of an account from wide open sea.
Just find a balance of sugar as wine is still bitter.
If I jump then I will try to fly and reach the horizon.
If I can't I will chase the horizon to stop it from distinction
It's all what I intend for inception.

RADNESWARY SOORIYAKUMAR JEGATHEESWARY

Radneswary is a young girl from Sri Lanka. Right now, she is reading her Bachelor's degree in Information Technology. Writing has always brought her immense happiness. Now she is here to explore more of her writings.
Insta id: raddy_rpss

Finally, the end is here
The last season of the year
Welcoming me with its chill

Winters are always amazing
The freezing snow falls
The early morning bliss

The short days and long nights
Are to start one moarcre time
The beginning of a new darkness

Now it's the snow flakes
Spread all over the dark floor
Looking as if they are painted

But this time it is different
Sitting all alone by the fire
Talking to myself of everything

This year hasn't been the same
So many has changed - Or
I've changed a lot

So many new meetups
So many new lessons
So many did I learn

Another year of experience
But sadly, with lots of pain
Handling all by myself

I've got to live alone
Be away from my ones
Stranded all alone here

This new journey of mine
In pursuing my career
Has brought me miles apart

Away from my family
Apart from my home
Now I've learnt to live

Just like the winter has come
Chilling out my warm blood
This new experience
Has taught me more.

SANANDA BHATTACHARJEE

This is Sananda Bhattacharjee, currently pursuing BA.LLB hons from Amity University Kolkata. She is born and brought up in Kolkata itself. She is a 21-year-old enthusiastic person. Her love towards writing started when she was in class 9. She has devoted herself into art and literature other than advocacy. She aims to influence a lot of people by providing a platform to explore their talents within them and that's why she founded "ENTANGLED TALES" which provides a platform to all to showcase their creativity. She believes that love and encouragement can bring out the best in one and aspires and inspires others towards the same motto.

And she chose not to limit her flight
To the subdued corners of her mind
To which she once was confined
For she envisions her canvas now
As the beautiful pink and lilac sky

And so, she plucked those broken quills
And dipped them in the myriad hues
Of her poems tranquil
And coloured lilac her gossamer wings
Creating the most beautiful masterpiece
From the broken palette of her confined dreams!

RASHMI MAURYA

Rashmi Maurya is a passionate writer who love to express human emotions in her words. She writes quotes, micro-fiction, poetries and blogs. She has YouTube channel with name (_the_poetry_zone) where she recites poetries written by her in Hindi and English.

I always found myself lost in the darkness
Fed up with disappointments and under the burdens of others'
expectations,
I was always considering myself not worthy of light even
Then I met a stranger in the mess of my life and he calls me his
angel
Who enlightened his lost track of life
I was never aware I will ever be able to get even good vibes
And he! he calls me his brightest light
I always felt if I don't fit anywhere or with anybody
That means the problem is within me
But he calls me the whole new dimension of his improvement
I highly doubted on all of my imagination
that those will ever be my reality
Then he called, called me as his only identity
I always felt maybe I over love
and would never be able to get it back as I deserve
I never found how to be the part of someone's life
Without being a burden
As this is how I always have been treated by all my so-called
closed ones
Then he happened and changed the whole definition
He sets me free because he thinks I am an angle
And I meant to live under the sky full of freedom.
Now I know what is the meaning of true happiness
Now I really know how to love my own self
Well I am still not sure that AM I eligible to be called an Angel
or not
But I do know that I finally have my worth
Nothing was wrong ever it was just me
Trying to fit in the place which was never mine
Now I do know that place called "my home" exists and it just
belongs to me!
Now I can say with my whole heart that I finally found my
paradise

MANISHA SHARMA

Manisha Sharma from Pali Rajasthan is an Assistant Professor in Commerce and management studies by Profession and a Writer by Passion. She is pursuing her PhD in Accounting. She is co-author of various anthologies. She believes that "Either write something worth reading or do something worth writing." You never have to change anything you got up in the middle of the night to write. Her Instagram handles are @manisha_sharma1729 and @sachhi_kalam1709. You can contact her on manishasharma1729@yahoo.com Keep reading.

सफर में मुश्किलें तो होगी,
जो चल सको तो चलो।
सभी है भीड़ में,
तुम भी निकल सको तो चलो।
किसी के वास्ते राहें कहाँ बदलती है,
तुम मुश्किलों से लड़ना सीख सको तो चलो।
मंजिल यूँ ही नहीं मिलती राही को,
एक जुनून सा दिल मे जगाना पड़ता है।
पूछा चिड़िया से की घोसला कैसे बनता है,
वो बोली तिनका- तिनका उठाना पड़ता है।
तू कोशिश कर तो हल निकलेगा,
आज नहीं तो कल निकलेगा।
मेहनत कर, पौधों को पानी दें,
बंजर जमीन से भी फल निकलेगा।
ज़िंदा रख दिमाग में सपनों को,
समंदर से भी गंगा जल निकलेगा।
कोशिशें जारी रख कुछ कर गजरने की,
जो आज थमा-थमा सा है,
वो आज नहीं तो कल चल निकलेगा,
वो आज नहीं तो कल चल निकलेगा।।

AHANA DEBNATH

Ahana Debnath is pursuing a Bachelor's Degree in English from Jadavpur University, Kolkata currently in her second year. Ahana aspires to be the Editor-in-chief of a prestigious publishing house. Reading and photography are two things she is passionate about. She is diligent and responsible, working towards fulfilling her dreams. She hopes someday to be worthy of Hemingway's famous quote, "There is nothing to writing. All you do is sit down at a typewriter and bleed." only on a laptop or computer.

These days we wake up with nowhere to be,
Dazed and disorientated stumbling from dreams to reality.
Don't know how long we keep staring at our ceilings,
Our heads filled with thoughts of despair, the sense of time
losing its meaning.
The gnawing fear of losing the ones we love slowly creeps
into our every waking moment,
Playing worst case scenarios over and over, our minds
becoming an invincible opponent.
Staying cooped up with a broken family is a new challenge,
Even though words cut deeper wounds they don't leave
visible scars to measure the damage.
Some of us wish we didn't have to wake up once the relief of
sleep came to the rescue.
But even in that we're plagued with nightmares, our demons
making our worst horrors come true.
We never finish our plates, our appetites lost,
Worrying about our families knowing not all of them will
making it out alive, free of cost.
Try as we might, it's impossible to concentrate on even
something we love, for too long,
along with losing touch with the people to whom we belong.
We don't remember the last time we laughed heartily at a
joke cracked by our friends,
Smiling seems like a crime when we see the suffering all
around that never seems to end.
Aimlessly wandering in our heads trying to salvage what's
left of our sanity,
Holding on to memories keeping us tethered from falling into
complete insanity.
Every day we remember a little less of what it was like
before all this,
The hope of a normal life slipping from our fingers ceasing
to exist.

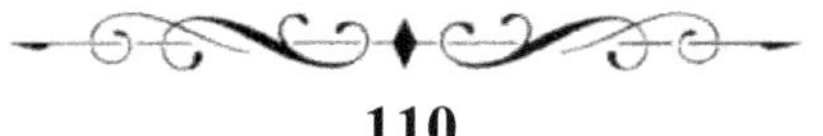

AASHIFA R

Aashifa is an outspoken extrovert, embracing the infinite shades of life. She is an engineer who held a job as a software developer until 2019. The 9-5 job added monotony to her burning desires and budding dreams and hence she quit and pursued freelancing and blogging. Now her blog (www.shi-sapien.com) is giving her the creative freedom to build an enthusiastic profession.

Age of Information, they say!
Snowballing freedom, they say!
A torrent of choices, they say!
Hurrah! The plethora of floating chances,
Are tangible, indeed!
But intangible,
Betwixt by a ghostly essence of reality,
Glued to the web spun by –
Myths & shams,
Fallacies & mendacity,
Palpable, yes!
Yet abstract,
Tugged into a pyrrhic void,
Hauled into an endless loop –
Tuned by the delusions and deceptions,
Fictions & fabrications –
Of those deceptive dancers,
Seated as devious negotiators,
Amidst the elegance of,
The pseudo-cultured debate rooms;
Ah! That joker's club,
And their noisy protocols,
Spinning truth,
Endorsing shade,
Converting this age of information,
Into an epoch of big lies.
Half of me tussle to lead a bastion of change…
Against the echoing lies of,
The well-fabricated crusade;
The other half of me desire to pacify & crystallize,
And delve into peace through poetry,
With some noise filters, of course!

SWARNASANKHA ACHARJEE

Swarnasankha Acharjee
Completed B.Sc. (Hons.) in Biomedical Science from
University of Delhi
Born and brought up in Tripura.

It's been a long time
She still looks sublime
Her hairs still flaunt
Her words still do haunt

It's been a long time
She still looks Hime
Her eyes still deep enough
To drown out all the stuff

Her grey turned eyebrows
Once looked dark as the crows
Her lips can still attract
Even the biggest of the bureaucrat

It's been a long time
She still looks Hime
She still possesses the feeling of jealousy
But that probably is our biggest Hennessy

It's been sixty years
Spent together in smiles and tears
It's been a journey of convincing and fighting
It's been a journey of loving and uniting

It's been a long time
She still looks sublime
Into the eighties she goes
Still looks as beautiful as a Rose!

Flairs and Glairs, a platform by a student for the students. We are esteemed youth struggling to carve out our path for our future and we follow a basic mindset Since everyone is not born with all-round skills. Joining hands with people who are born to execute it with perfection is the best way to evolve. Self-Evolution is the need of the hour but, evolving as a community is what we strive for. The initiative as kickstarted by, Founder- Mr. Shubham Shah with the motive to utilize the skillset and talent of writing has now a team of 10+ people who are actively participating into newer forms of learning and discovering talents among youngsters. We Provide platform and services like Publishing opportunities, Open mics, Workshops, Hands-on training. Operating with Brand Name of Flairs and Glairs (Publication House), we offer the chance of elevating a passionate writer to an esteemed author With Brand name Teekhe Zasbaaat. We bring to you an opportunity to get accustomed with the Public Speaking and Presenting of Thoughts along with regular challenges to brush up your inking spirit. The newest initiative to extend our services we introduced in a new writing Platform- The Glittering Fables and Ink Over Tears.

We Choose to Fly Like A Falcon than to be a Leg Pulling Crab.

To Know More: Infoline – 7781900870
Mail Us At-
flairsandglairs@gmail.com / info@flairsandglairs.in
Or Visit is at
www.flairsandglairs.com / www.flairsandglairs.in
Social Handles- @flairsandglairs @teekhezasbaaat